DAMIAN DROOTH
SUPERSLEUTH

MEGA QUIZ

DAMIAN DROOTH
SUPERSLEUTH

MEGA QUIZ

BARBARA MITCHELHILL

Illustrated by TONY ROSS

ANDERSEN PRESS
LONDON

First published in 2015 by
Andersen Press Limited
20 Vauxhall Bridge Road
London SW1V 2SA
www.andersenpress.co.uk

2 4 6 8 10 9 7 5 3 1

The right of Barbara Mitchelhill and Tony Ross to be identified as
the author and illustrator of this work has been asserted by them in
accordance with the Copyright, Designs and Patents Act, 1988.

Text copyright © Barbara Mitchelhill, 2015
Illustrations copyright © Tony Ross, 2015

British Library Cataloguing in Publication Data available.

ISBN 978 1 78344 258 4

Printed and bound by CPI Group
(UK) Ltd, Croydon, CR0 4YY

Chapter 1

My name is Drooth. Damian Drooth, boy detective and all-round genius. Inspector Crockitt, the head of the local police, is amazed at my crime-busting skills.

For instance, last week I solved a really difficult case. It started like this: on Saturday morning, I was in the library borrowing a book about my hero, Sherlock Holmes. I'd chosen one called *The Hound of the Baskervilles* and was walking out of the library when I noticed a poster on the wall. This is what it said:

Do you have a brilliant brain?
Are you between 10 and 12 years old?

WIN A WEEKEND IN
DISNEYLAND PARIS

Enter our Mega Quiz
Teams of 4
Entrance fee: £10 each
Fill in the form below and post back

Interesting, I thought. So I picked up a form and called a meeting of my trainee detectives. This gang was made up of Tod and his sister Lavender (who was only six but quite bright for a girl), Harry (who was not brilliant but was taller than any of us) and Winston (who was great at karate).

That afternoon, they all came to the hut at the bottom of my garden.

'What now, Damian?' asked Tod. 'Have you spotted another crime?'

I didn't answer. I stood on a stool so everybody could see me, like Mr Spratt, our headmaster, when he stands on the stage in assembly.

I spoke in my loudest voice. 'How would you like to go to Disneyland Paris?'

Their mouths fell open with shock. Then I explained about the Mega Quiz.

'It's simple,' I said. 'We know loads of stuff, so we'll win, easy.'

Harry looked worried. 'I don't know much,' he said. 'Can't Lavender go instead of me?'

'No. She's only six,' I told him. 'Don't worry, we've got two weeks before the quiz. We'll go down to the library to study. I bet Miss Travis will be pleased to see us.'

'She wasn't pleased the last time we went,' said Harry.

'That was because we took Curly with us,' I said. 'She's not keen on dogs, especially in the library.'

I noticed Tod was frowning. 'Studying is a good idea,' he said.  'But how do we get the money for the entrance fees? Ten pounds each is forty pounds.'

Tod was good at maths so I guessed that he was right.

'I got ten pounds for my birthday,' said Winston. 'We can use that.'

'I've got thwee pounds in my piggy bank,' said Lavender, 'and there's a pound coin in my purthe.'

Things were looking up.

'How about you, Harry?' I asked. 'Have you got any money?'

'Only what I'm saving for my bike. I can't spend that.'

I didn't see why not. 'You mean you don't want to go to Disneyland Paris with us?'

He pulled a funny face and sighed. 'I do but…'

'So how much have you saved?'

'Twelve pounds.'

'We still need … er …' I said.

Then Smarty Pants Tod butted in. 'Fourteen pounds,' he said, obviously wanting everybody to know that he was the All-Time Maths Genius.

After that, we sat in the shed trying to work out how to get fourteen pounds.

It was Lavender who spoke up. 'We could do jobths,' she said.

'What kind of jobs?' I asked.

'Wathing cars, gardening, taking dogths for walkths.'

Sometimes Lavender comes up with excellent ideas.

'Good thinking,' I said. 'We'll soon earn fourteen pounds. Let's do it.'

Chapter 2

The gang went home and I walked back up the garden and into the kitchen which was filled with the fantastic smell of baking. Mum has her own business, Home Cooking Unlimited. She's really good – especially her chocolate gateau, which is *AWESOME!*

That afternoon, there were some cupcakes on the table, just out of the oven and waiting to be decorated. I had an idea. If I decorated them, Mum would be really pleased and would probably pay me. I'd never done it before but I'd watched her do it plenty of times. How hard could it be to squeeze butter icing out of a piping bag? Easy-peasy!

First, I got the butter and icing sugar. But the butter was rock hard from the fridge and, when I tried to mix the two together, the icing sugar puffed up like white smoke. I coughed. I choked. So I ate one of the cupcakes to soothe my throat – even though I prefer chocolate cakes myself.

Then a brilliant idea popped into my head. If I mixed cocoa powder with the butter icing, I could make it chocolate flavoured. I grabbed a chair and climbed up to reach the top shelf of the cupboard where Mum kept the tin of cocoa. But the chair wasn't very steady. It wobbled. The tin flew out of my hand and the cocoa went everywhere. Some went over me but most went on the kitchen floor.

Not to worry! I scooped it up with a spoon and mixed it with the butter icing. There were a few black bits in it and I had to pick out a dead fly – but I didn't think anyone would notice. Anyway, the mixture had turned brown – so that was good. Once I'd spooned it into the piping bag, I squeezed it over the cupcakes – which wasn't easy owing to some little lumps, which might have been the butter, I suppose.

There wasn't enough butter icing to cover all of the cakes – three were left without topping, so I thought it best to eat them.

I could hardly wait for Mum to see my fabulous display. But when she walked in, I didn't get the reaction I'd expected.

'What on earth have you been up to, Damian?' she asked, pointing to the cocoa powder on the floor (even though I'd picked most of it up). 'What's that mess?'

I pretended not to hear. Instead, I pointed to the cupcakes. I thought she'd be pleased – but she wasn't.

When she saw them, her eyes bulged like marbles. 'You've ruined my

cupcakes!' she shouted. 'They were for a
little girl's birthday party this afternoon.'
She bent over the kitchen table to get a
closer look. 'What have you put on the
top of them?'

'Chocolate butter icing,' I said –
although I thought any cook would
know that.

Her cheeks went scarlet. 'She wanted
pink, Damian! NOT BROWN!'

THEN she spotted a small spider (it was dead) on top of one of the cakes and she went mad! She was in such a bad mood there was no point in asking her to pay me. I did what I always do. I left the house and went round to see Harry.

Chapter 3

On the way to Harry's house, I bumped into Tod, who had two dogs on leads – Blossom (Mrs Popperwell's poodle) and Curly (Tod's own dog).

'Mrs Popperwell's paying me a pound to take Blossom round the park,' he said. 'Dad said I had to take Curly at the same time.'

'Two pounds, eh? Not bad.'

'No! Not two pounds! Dad said that cos Curly's my dog, I shouldn't get paid for taking her for a walk.'

Shame! But still, a pound was better than nothing, I thought.

Then Tod gave me a funny look. 'Why have you got brown stuff on your sweater?'

'A bit of an accident in the kitchen,' I said. 'Mum went into a tizz about it, so I'm going to see Harry.'

'He's not at home, Damian. He's doing jobs for Mrs Popperwell.'

This was good news. Mrs Popperwell has always been grateful for me saving Blossom from the Dog Snatcher. She usually gives us drinks and biscuits.

'I'll go round then,' I said, just as Blossom and Curly spotted a cat and dragged Tod away down the road.

I found Harry at the front of Mrs Popperwell's house, cleaning the living-room window.

'Keep up the good work, Harry!' I said. 'I'm going inside to say hello to Mrs Popperwell.'

I was soon sitting in a comfy chair with a slice of Mrs Popperwell's cherry cake and some home-made lemonade. I waved to Harry, who was sloshing water on the window and looked very wet.

'I'm impressed that you boys are working hard to earn some money,' said Mrs Popperwell. 'Winston is out in the back garden weeding the flower beds.'

It was great to hear that he was doing his bit too. Good old Winston!

Mrs Popperwell gave me one of her grandmotherly smiles. 'What about you, Damian? What are you going to do?'

I explained how I had tried to help Mum but it hadn't worked out because she was in a bit of a mood.

'I expect she was tired,' she said. 'Never mind, dear. You can help Winston. There are lots of weeds to pull out.'

Gardening wasn't my thing. I didn't like digging and stuff. But I went out anyway. Winston tried to explain which were weeds and which were plants. I couldn't see the difference myself.

I hadn't been there long when Harry came round the back. 'I've finished the windows. Mrs Popperwell's paying me a pound a window,' he said. 'And I've done five.'

'That's brilliant, Harry!' I said. 'But there's more than five.'

He shook his head. 'Mrs Popperwell said it's too dangerous to do the bedroom windows.'

'But I bet she'll be pleased if you did them,' I replied. 'There's a ladder behind the shed. Why don't we go and get it?'

Harry soon saw the sense of it. 'All right,' he said. 'I'll do it.'

I offered to hold the ladder. It was the least I could do.

Harry climbed up and started on the bedroom window while I waited at the bottom. But just as he was reaching over for the final polish, the ladder slipped sideways.

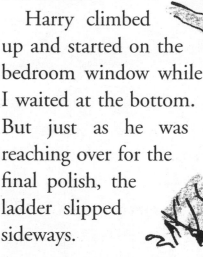

'Aaaagh!' screamed Harry.

'Look out!' I shouted as he fell. 'Mind the rose bushes, Harry!' They were Mrs Popperwell's pride and joy.

Too late. Harry landed right in the middle. He lay there, groaning and yelling. No wonder. Roses have loads of thorns.

'Wait there!' I said and ran to fetch Mrs Popperwell.

When she saw Harry, she cried, 'Oh my goodness! I must call the ambulance at once.'

Two men came and put him onto a stretcher and carried him into the ambulance. Winston and I jumped into Mrs Popperwell's car and she followed the ambulance with its blue light flashing and its siren blaring. It was really, really exciting – like one of the cop programmes on the telly. We zoomed down the road at top speed. Traffic screeched to a halt and let us pass as we headed in the direction of the hospital.

'Good driving, Mrs Popperwell!' I called from the back seat. 'You could be in the Grand Prix!'

Once we were there, we had to wait in the corridor while they put Harry's leg in plaster. It would have been interesting to see how they did it, but they wouldn't let us watch. When they let him out, Winston and me were the first to sign the plaster cast. Best of all, he got a pair of crutches.

Mrs Popperwell was still upset. 'It was my fault,' she said, wiping the tears from her cheeks. 'I should never have let you clean the windows, Harry.'

Just to make up for it, she was very generous when she paid us all for the work we'd done.

'Thanks, Mrs Popperwell,' I said. 'Now we'll be able to enter the quiz.'

Chapter 4

When we met in the shed the next day, Tod was in a sulk cos he'd missed all the excitement of going to hospital. But he was OK when Harry said he could sign his cast. Lavender did a drawing of a cat which was quite good.

We decided that she should fill in the form for the quiz cos she had the best writing. Then we put the money into an envelope and Lavender wrote the address on the front.

'Now we'd better start some serious studying,' I said. 'It's only a week before the Mega Quiz.'

It was too far for Harry to walk to the library on his crutches, so Winston fetched the buggy he'd made last year and we took it in turns to pull him along. When we arrived, Miss Travis, the librarian, was shocked to see Harry's injury.

'How did he do it, Damian?' she asked.

'He was doing work for charity,' I said – which was a bit of a lie, I admit. But Miss Travis was *IMPRESSED!*

'We're here to study,' I told her and she was even *MORE IMPRESSED!*

She took us over to a table tucked away in the far corner. 'Nobody will disturb you here. I don't want anyone bumping into this poor boy.' She smiled and gave Harry a pat on his shoulder. She even let him put the buggy under the table.

That table was the best in the library cos nobody could see us. It meant we could eat sandwiches and crisps – which was the best way to increase our brain power.

Every afternoon after that, we went to study. We each had our own specialist subjects. Winston's was dinosaurs, Harry's was football, Tod's was geography, history, maths and science. Mine was Sherlock Holmes books. Lavender just sat in the corner reading her favourite stories. We had a few complaints from Miss Travis about crumbs and crisps on the floor and not putting the books away. But she never shouted. I think Harry's injury made all the difference.

On the Saturday that the Mega Quiz was to be held in the Town Hall, we met in the shed. I gave a team talk just like football managers do before a big match.

'We're going to win this quiz,' I said. 'Just think positive, get your brains in gear and we'll soon be on our way to Disneyland Paris.'

'You're tho good, Damian,' said Lavender. 'I'll be there in the audienth to cheer you on.' She'd even brought a flag to wave. Good old Lavender!

We set off in good time. Harry said he could manage now on his crutches – so that meant we didn't have to take the buggy.

By the time we were in the middle of town, we were amazed to see a procession with a brass band in blue uniform marching down towards the Town Hall.

The Mayor was at the front wearing his gold chain. Lots of people were following behind and I spotted Dixie Stanton and Annabelle Harrington-Smythe* among them. So they had entered the quiz, had they? Well, they didn't stand a chance of winning with us in the competition.

'TV reporters are here with their cameras,' I said to the others. 'This quiz must be more important than I thought.

*Two girls from our school: Dixie Stanton was a real pain. Annabelle had blonde hair and blue eyes. She was OK.

We'd better join the back of the parade, quick.'

The procession went inside the Town Hall, which was very grand with a great wide staircase leading up to a massive wood-panelled hall.

'Look,' said Tod as we walked in. 'Your mum's over there.'

Sure enough, Mum was standing behind a row of tables covered in white cloths and spread with plates of sandwiches, sausage rolls and a variety of

cakes. She was pouring tea from a huge teapot into china cups.

'Did you know she'd be here, Damian?' asked Winston.

'She might have mentioned it,' I said, 'but I've been busy studying, haven't I?'

I didn't want Mum to see me. Luckily, there were so many people helping themselves to the food that she didn't spot me. Thank goodness. Since the incident with the cupcakes, she'd been in a terrible mood.

'I'm glad they're feeding us before the quiz,' said Winston as he bit into his third sausage roll.

'Eat as much as you can,' I said. 'It's good brain food.'

When everybody had finished, the Mayor stepped up on to the stage.

'Great!' I said. 'The quiz is starting.'

The Mayor took hold of a microphone but, instead of announcing the Mega Quiz, he began a very long, boring speech about cabbages and carrots. I ask you! What's that got to do with the quiz? We'd never get to Disneyland Paris at this rate, I thought. I was very patient. I waited and waited but he didn't mention the Mega Quiz once. He even gave somebody a silver cup for growing tomatoes.

By then, it was two o'clock and he was still speechifying. I had to do something! I found a chair and stood on it so that I was a head above the crowd.

'Excuse me, Mr Mayor,' I called out in my loudest voice. 'How long is this speech going on? We're waiting to do the quiz.'

There was a gasp as everybody in the hall turned to look at me. I heard Mum shout, 'Damian? What are you doing here?' Then, before I knew it, three burly men in black suits grabbed hold of me, carried me down the stairs and threw me out of the building.

'It's not fair!' I yelled. 'We came for the Mega Quiz.'

One of them called back. 'There ain't no quiz, sonny. You've got it wrong. This is the Allotment Diggers' Annual Award.'

Chapter 5

I was sitting on the steps of the Town Hall rubbing my bruises, when the others came out to join me.

'Those men were rough,' I moaned. 'There was no need to throw me out.'

'Perwaps we got the time of the quiz wong, Damian,' said Lavender.

'No,' I said. 'I've worked it out. There isn't a quiz and we won't be going to Disneyland Paris. It's a scam*.'

Harry couldn't believe it. 'A scam? How do you work that out?'

'We've been tricked. Somebody's made a lot of money out of us.' I felt really bad. Me! Damian Drooth, boy detective and all-round genius! I had been fooled.

But I wasn't going to let the fraudster get away with it. 'We'd better go back

*A scam is a way of tricking people out of money.

to the library. I've got some important questions to ask Miss Travis.'

We marched back across town to the library where a line of people were queuing at the desk, waiting to take books out.

'Excuse me!' I called as I pushed my way to the front. 'This is an emergency.'

Miss Travis looked up. 'What is it, Damian? I'm very busy.'

I leaned across the desk. 'We found a poster for a quiz in the library and it's a fake. A big CON! We lost forty pounds!'

Miss Travis's mouth fell open and she clapped her hands to her cheeks. 'Oh my goodness,' she said. 'I'm afraid somebody put it up without asking. I took it down last week. I'm sorry if you've been cheated out of your money. I think you should tell the police.'

I had no intention of telling the police. I'm much better on my own in the crime-busting business.

'So what do we do next?' Harry asked.

'We've got to find out where this criminal lives,' I replied. 'But it's not going to be easy.'

'I know where he livth,' Lavender said.

I stared at her. 'How do you know that?'

'I wote it on the envelope,' she said. 'I can wemember it.'

Lavender never fails to amaze me.

When she's a bit older, she'll make a first-class detective.

I gave her a pen and this is what she wrote in my notebook: Mr Smith, 154 Clayton Road, Broxley.

'Broxley's only five miles away,' I said. 'Come on. We'll catch the bus.'

Luckily Harry's uncle had given him some money for being brave when he broke his leg and it was enough for all our fares.

'We must put disguises in our backpacks,' I said before we left. 'You never know if we'll need them.'

And then we set off.

Chapter 6

On the bus, I explained my plan. 'I'll go to his house and speak to Mr Smith – but I don't suppose that's his real name.'

'What if he's dangerous?' asked Tod.

'In my experience,' I said, 'criminals are very nervous if they think they've been sussed*. Don't worry. We'll stand together.'

The bus dropped us off outside number 154, which wasn't a house at all. It was a newsagent's shop.

'I expect Mr Smith bought it with all the money he's stolen,' I said. 'But he won't get away. I've got a Plan B.'

'What's Plan B?' asked Harry.

'I go into the shop and look around for clues.'

'Won't that look suspicious?'

'Not if I buy some sweets,' I explained.

*Detectives' language meaning 'found out'.

'Got any money left, Harry?'

When I walked in the newsagent's, a lady in a red and gold sari was standing behind the counter. She didn't look like a criminal. Maybe her husband was the criminal and he was hiding in the back.

As I glanced round looking for clues, I spotted six pigeonholes behind the counter. Each one had a name over the top – Mrs Beddows, Mr O'Malley – that kind of thing. Being a detective, I knew that people had their letters sent to places like this when they wanted to keep things secret.

Five of the pigeonholes were empty but the sixth had letters in it and this was labelled 'MR SMITH'! Interesting, I thought.

Staying cool, I bought a bag of sweets and then I leaned on the counter and smiled my most friendly smile.

'I notice you take in letters for people,'
I said as I popped a sweet into my mouth.

'Yes,' the lady replied. 'They call in
each morning to pick up their mail.'

'But not Mr Smith,' I said, pointing
to the last pigeonhole.

The lady looked at her watch and smiled. 'We close in an hour's time, but I'm sure he'll be here before then. He gets a lot of letters.'

Before I could ask more questions, two women with a baby in a pushchair came into the shop – so I left and shared the information with the gang as well as the bag of sweets.

'It shouldn't be long before the fraudster turns up,' I said, chewing on a humbug. 'We'll just hang around and wait.'

'But we don't know what he looks like,' said Tod.

I sighed. 'I explained ages ago how to spot criminal types. Anyone with eyes close together and with a beard – especially a black one – is certain to be up to no good. Make sure you remember that!'

I gave the gang more instructions. Tod and Winston were to stand on one side of the shop door while Harry, Lavender and me were on the other. We'd hardly finished dishing out the sweets when Lavender suddenly squealed, 'A manth's coming up the stweet. He hath a black beard.'

We all turned to look.

'Good work, Lavender,' I said. 'Get ready for action, team!'

Unfortunately, the man walked right past us, past the shop and on up the street.

'That wasn't Mr Smith, was it, Damian?' said Winston.

I shook my head. 'No. The beard was too small.'

'But you thaid to look for a black beard,' said Lavender as tears rolled down her cheeks.

'Small beards don't count,' I explained. 'But nice try, Lavender.'

After that, I thought it would be better if I kept a lookout for criminal types. And I soon spotted a man with a large black beard and eyes fixed close together.

'This is him,' I hissed. 'Watch and learn.'

I don't think he even noticed me as he headed towards the shop. I gave Harry a signal to stick out one of his crutches. The fraudster didn't see it, of course, and went flying head over heels.

'What the—' he yelled as he landed face down on the floor.

'Don't move,' I called out while Tod sat on him and Winston stood near, ready to deliver a karate chop if necessary.

'Send for the police,' I shouted to the shopkeeper. 'Ask for Inspector Crockitt. This man is a criminal. He runs the Mega Quiz and he stole our money.'

But the shopkeeper didn't pick up the phone. 'You stupid boy!' she shouted. 'He doesn't run any quiz. That's Mr O'Leary and he's come to collect his newspaper.'

He was making terrible noises.
'Aaaagh! Ooooh! Wooooow!' he yelled.
'You've damaged my back! I'll have the
Law on you.'

I tried to help him up. I even offered
him a sweet, but he refused.

The shopkeeper shouted, 'Get out
of here!' and pointed to the door. She
followed us out onto the pavement,
shaking her fist and making sure we
walked well away from the shop.

'What do we do now, Damian?' asked Winston.

'Plan C.'

'What's Plan C?'

'We'll go back and wait for the real criminal.'

'That's not Plan C!' said Tod. 'That's just the same as Plan B. Anyway, we daren't go near the shop again. '

'Plan C is different,' I told him. 'We'll put on disguises so nobody will recognise us. You can play your guitar, Tod. Harry – get out your mouth organ. We're going to busk.'

Chapter 7

My disguise was a hat, a black coat and shades. Tod had his Mexican outfit and Lavender was Snow White. Nobody would recognise us – especially Harry, who had brought a false beard along.

My plan was simple: we'd walk back up the road and busk outside Quick Cuts, the hairdresser's. It was opposite the newsagent's shop so we could keep a lookout for the fraudster who was sure to arrive before the shop closed.

As Tod took his guitar from his backpack, he shook his head. 'I can't play it, Damian. A couple of strings have broken.'

'Don't worry,' I said. 'Just play the strings that are OK. Nobody will notice.'

Once we were outside Quick Cuts, Tod and Harry started to play. Winston and I sang as loud as we could to cover up some peculiar notes coming from Tod's guitar and I thought it sounded pretty good.

'What about me, Damian?' asked Lavender. 'Shall I sing too?'

But I didn't think a girl fitted into a boy band, so I told her to skip up and down the road for a bit.

The ladies who were having their hair done seemed to enjoy our music. They looked out of the window smiling and waving at us. But before long the hairdresser came marching out of the shop, yelling and brandishing a pair of scissors.

'Stop that terrible noise right now! You're disturbing my customers. If you don't stop it, I'll report you!' Then she turned round and walked back inside.

I was amazed. She didn't seem to appreciate our music at all. I moved the gang a few metres down the road. 'Keep playing,' I said. 'It sounds great! With a bit more practice we could be number one in the charts.'

I was enjoying myself so much that I was seriously thinking of turning to pop music as my future career. But then Lavender came tugging at my sleeve.

'Damian! Damian!' she shouted, so loudly that I had to stop singing.

'What is it?'

'I've theen Mr Thmith. Quick! He'th gone into the newthagenth.'

Lavender had got it wrong before, so I wasn't sure I could believe her. 'Has he got a big black beard?'

'No, he hathn't got any hair at all. He'th bald but...'

'Then he can't be Mr Smith, can he?' I said, giving the signal for the gang to start playing again.

But Lavender was determined. 'Look, Damian,' she said, pushing some leaflets into my hand. 'They dwopped out of hith bag.'

I looked at them and was amazed to see that they were advertising the Mega Quiz!

'Good work, Lavender. He's Mr Smith, for sure!' I said.

I turned to the others. 'I'm going into the newsagent's shop.'

'No! It'th dangerwuth,' said Lavender.

I shrugged. 'A detective's life is full of danger, Lavender. The rest of you stay here, ready for action.'

Wearing my disguise, I slipped into the shop and hid behind a tall display of birthday cards. Mr Smith was talking to the shopkeeper.

'I'll take my letters, if you please, Mrs Malik,' he said, 'but I shan't need your services after today. I'm leaving town.'

This was a terrible shock. I had to act now. If I didn't, he'd be gone and he'd escape the Law.

I crouched down and I began to crawl out from my hiding place. I went silently across the shop floor until I was behind the fraudster. Then I reached forward, got hold of his shoelaces and tied them together. Once I'd done that, I pulled my whistle out of my top pocket and blew hard – which was the signal for my detective gang to come.

When the criminal heard the whistle, he spun round but, with his feet tied, he couldn't move.

The gang came running towards him. He crashed to the floor and, while they made sure he didn't get up, I dialled 999.

'You young hooligans!' Smith yelled. 'What are you doing?'

'You're nicked!' I said, showing him the posters. 'The Mega Quiz is a scam.'

Then he knew the game was up and he lay quivering on the floor.

But only seconds later, I was amazed to see the police burst into the shop, led by Inspector Crockitt.

'That was quick,' I said. 'We've only just caught him.'

The inspector didn't look pleased. I expect he wanted to catch the criminal himself.

'Oh, it's you, Damian,' he said. 'The hairdresser from Quick Cuts called us and said there was a gang of kids terrorising the neighbourhood. I should have known you were involved.'

I must say I felt rather hurt. But when I explained that I'd tracked down a villain who was running a money-making scam – well, he apologised.

Even the shopkeeper apologised and gave us a bag of sweets each and some chocolate. Not bad for a day's work.

Chapter 8

I had learned a lot from reading the Sherlock Holmes books. I had solved another crime and put a nasty criminal behind bars. Even Mum was pleased with me this time and she forgot about the cupcakes.

It turned out that the Mega Quiz scam had conned loads of kids like us. Everybody got their money back in the end and the fraudster was dragged away to prison. Job done!

Mr Spratt, our headmaster, told the whole school about it.

'Damian and his friends did very well to catch the man responsible,' he said. 'But they missed out on a chance to enter a quiz so I thought we should have one in school.'

This was brilliant – although I was disappointed that he didn't mention going to Disneyland Paris.

The headmaster looked around the hall. 'Now who will make up a team to compete with Damian's?'

Straight away, Dixie Stanton jumped to her feet (worse luck!). 'It could be boys against girls, sir. I'll get a girls' team together. Some of my friends are really brainy.'

This sounded bad. I didn't like having anything to do with Dixie Stanton. The only good thing was that she was friends with Annabelle Harrington-Smythe. She was OK.

*

The following week, the quiz was held in the hall. The Mayor came with his big gold chain, our families were invited and Mrs Popperwell came with Inspector Crockitt. Mrs P is Inspector Crockitt's auntie and she makes sure he appreciates me (which he doesn't always).

Each round of the quiz was on a topic. We won the football and the dinosaur rounds. The girls won history (so much

for Tod studying that one!) and the wildlife round as we didn't know much about birds and that. So far it was two rounds each.

'The final round,' Mr Spratt announced, 'is on books.'

Harry and Winston didn't look pleased. Only Tod looked confident. The girls were smirking. They thought they were in with a good chance.

Mr Spratt said, 'I want you to write down the authors of the following books. One: *Harry Potter and the Philosopher's Stone,* two: *War Horse,* three: *The Tale of Peter Rabbit* and four: *Oliver Twist.*'*

Tod wasn't sure of two of them. Now it all depended on how good the girls were. I thought Annabelle would probably be brilliant.

We handed the paper in and Mr Spratt looked at the answers. 'Well, well, well. Each team has only two answers correct so I shall have to ask a final question which will decide the winner of the competition.'

We all chewed our pencils, waiting for him to speak.

'Who was the author of the books about Sherlock Holmes?'

The girls looked blank and shook their heads. Dixie Stanton looked especially

*Answers: 1. J K Rowling 2. Michael Morpurgo 3. Beatrix Potter 4. Charles Dickens

miserable. I leaped
to my feet, arm in
the air. 'I know!
I know!'

I must admit
Mr Spratt looked
ever so surprised.
'Very well,
Damian. If you
think you know it, you'd better tell us.'

'I've read all the Sherlock books, sir.
That's why I catch criminals faster than
the police.'

I noticed that Inspector Crockitt
frowned and bit his lip but Mrs
Popperwell smiled and nodded in
agreement.

'So who is the author?'

I looked at the audience. 'Sir Arthur
Conan Doyle,' I said triumphantly and
everybody cheered. We had won!

There wasn't a trip to Disneyland but we did get a box of chocolates each and we celebrated afterwards with lemonade, sandwiches and cupcakes.

'You're wonderful, Damian,' said Mrs Popperwell and she nudged Inspector Crockitt. 'Isn't he clever, Brian?'

'Yes ... er ... Well done, Damian,' said Inspector Crockitt.

'Thanks,' I said. 'It's a question of brain power. Any time you want my help, just ask.'

DAMIAN DROOTH SUPERSLEUTH

ACE DETECTIVE

by Barbara Mitchelhill

with illustrations by
Tony Ross

Damian Drooth is a super sleuth, a number
one detective, a kid with a nose for trouble.
And here in this fantastic bumper edition are
three of his hilarious stories:
The Case of the
Disappearing Daughter,
How to Be a Detective
and The Case of the
Pop Star's Wedding.

'Madcap cartoon-
sketch humour'
TES

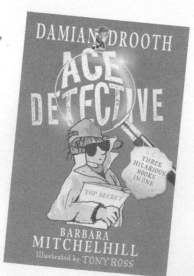

9781849390972 £6.99